Piggy-Bank Minds
and 49 Other Object Lessons for Children

Piggy-Bank Minds

and 49 Other Object Lessons for Children

Dorothy Brenner Francis

Abingdon • Nashville

Piggy-Bank Minds and 49
Other Object Lessons for Children

Copyright © 1977 by Abingdon

Second Printing 1978

Library of Congress Cataloging in Publication Data

FRANCIS, DOROTHY BRENNER.
  Piggy-bank minds and 49 other object lessons for
children.
  1. Children's sermons. I. Title.
BV4315.F64   252'.53   76-49639

ISBN 0-687-31420-8

MANUFACTURED   BY   THE   PARTHENON   PRESS   AT
NASHVILLE, TENNESSEE, UNITED STATES OF AMERICA

For Ann and Pat

Contents

King for a Lifetime

Props: *A cardboard crown, a flower, a weed.*

Did you know that you are a king? You didn't?
Well, it's true. I can guess what you're thinking.
You're probably thinking that your mother and
father are king and queen in your family. And your
teacher seems like king of the schoolroom. The big
kids are kings of the playground, and for sure your
baby brother is king of the nursery.

How many of you have a baby brother or sister?
Do you sometimes feel that the baby wears the
crown in your family? People fuss over babies. They
bring them gifts. They give them lots of attention. All
that is true, but those things don't make your own
crown lopsided. Not at all.

Just feel up there on your head. Don't you feel
that crown? You don't? You don't think you're king
of anything? Listen and I'll tell you something
special.

Each one of you is king over his own thoughts.
Think about that. It's really true. You are king of
your own mind. You're the boss of what thoughts
shall enter your mind, and you're the boss of what
thoughts will stay there.

Your thought-kingdom is really important, because thoughts can make you happy or they can
make you unhappy. You may not have thought
much about your mind. How many of you sit

around thinking about your mind? Not many people do.

How many of you have gardens at home? Good. It may help you to understand your mind-kingdom if you'll think of your mind as a garden. Do you know what this is? (Hold up a petunia.) Sure, it's a petunia. Petunias make a garden beautiful. Every king should plant a few petunias in his mind-garden.

Do you know what this is? (Hold up a weed.) Right. It's a thistle, a weed. Weeds are troublesome. What does a gardener do with weeds? Right. He pulls them up.

Since you are king of your own mind-garden, it will be up to you to pull out the ugly thought-weeds and to save the beautiful thought-flowers. What are some thought-weeds that you'll want to get rid of? Hating. Selfishness. Jealousy. And what are some thought-flowers that you kings will want to encourage? Kindness. Sharing. Loving.

Always remember that you are the king of your own mind. It's a big responsibility, but you can handle it. If your thoughts get tangled and out of control, you can always turn to God for help. He'll certainly understand your problems, for the Bible tells us that God is the king of kings.

Sentence prayer: Our Father: Help us to realize the importance of the kingdoms of mind, and give us grace to rule wisely. Amen.

Four Important Words

Prop: *A tall bean plant.*

Do you know the story of Jack and the beanstalk? You've heard about the magic bean seeds that grew into a huge beanstalk overnight? Sometimes don't you wish you were magic and could grow up overnight? People are always talking about being grown up, aren't they?

How many of you have had people ask you, "What do you want to be when you grow up?" I'll guess that all of you have heard that question from someone. And what's your answer? You have a lot of choices. A fire fighter? A police officer? A schoolteacher? What do you want to be? Do you have some ideas? (Let the children talk a bit.)

Those are all fine ideas, but there's something else to think about. How will you know when you've grown up? Will you be grown up when you're eighteen years old? Will you be grown up when you're as tall as your dad? Will you be grown up when you're as old as your Uncle Bill? How *will* you know when you're grown up? Will you get a letter from the president of the Loyal Order of Grown-ups saying, "Ta-Da! Today you are grown up"? I doubt it.

Let's consider this growing up business a bit more. If you have a younger brother or sister, you

11

probably hear two words quite often. "Help me." Isn't that right? Doesn't your little brother or sister come around a lot saying, "Help me tie my shoe." "Help me get a drink." Help me this. Help me that.

At the same time you hear all the help me's from the small fry you might be thinking, "I'm glad I can help myself." Do you ever think that? It's all right to think that. Being glad that you can help yourself is important because helping yourself is part of being grown up. When you can help yourself, you're on your way.

Now, maybe you don't say "Help me" much anymore. And maybe you say, "I can help myself." But there are four more important words for you to learn to use. You'll know you're really on your way to being grown up when you can say, "I can help others."

All of you can say that now and then. You're not going to grow up overnight like Jack's beanstalk. But you'll know you're making progress when you can say, "I can help my brother tie his shoe" or, "I can help my sister zip her jacket." How about thinking about those four words this week? See how many times you can stretch your age by saying, "I can help others."

Sentence prayer: Our Father: We thank you for the opportunity to help others, knowing you will guide us as we grow. Amen.

The Homemade Toy

Prop: *A homemade toy or doll.*

How many of you people like to make things? Maybe you like to make toys—a wagon, an airplane, or a miniature service station or farm. Let's hear from some of you. What have you made that you really like?

I want to show you something that I made a long time ago. What do you think of this? (Hold up the prop.) It's old, isn't it? And it looks as if it has had a lot of wear and tear. You can see that it's sort of lopsided. And the top was put on crooked. The paint's peeling in some spots, and where the paint isn't peeling it's fading.

As a child I saw all the scroungy things about this toy, but they weren't important to me. This was one of my favorite playthings. I entertained myself with it for many hours at a time. Oh, I had other toys that had been purchased at the store and were nicer and newer, but for some reason this one was my favorite. Do you ever feel that way about a toy you've made yourself? Do you ever feel that a toy you've made is your very favorite? You do? I wonder why that is. Why do you prefer a homemade toy to all your other toys?

I think I heard somebody whisper the answer I was thinking of. I like this old beat-up toy of mine just because I made it. Isn't that the way you feel

13

about the toys you've made? You like them in spite of all their faults, just because you made them with your own imagination and your own hands.

This thought can be very comforting. The Bible tells us that we are made in the image of God; so if we love our own creations—these silly-looking toys—then it stands to reason that God must love his creations—you and me. Isn't it good to know that our creator loves us in spite of all the things about us that aren't quite perfect?

When I was about your age there was a song that children sometimes sang. The words went something like this: "Nobody loves me. Everybody hates me. I'll go out and eat worms." Sometimes we all have moments when we feel that nobody loves us. I know I do. But instead of eating worms I just think of this old battered toy and how much I love it. And that reminds me that God loves me in spite of everything.

Sentence prayer: Our Father: We thank you for the gift of your love. Help us to deserve it. Amen.

Fall Leaves

Prop: *An array of leaves in all colors.*

Have you all noticed how pretty the leaves are this fall? If you haven't noticed, just look around you when you leave here today. Some trees are decked out in scarlet. Others are golden yellow. A few will be brown, and a few more will still be green. This contrast of colors is one of the beauties of the fall season.

You may think the scarlet leaves on the maple tree in your yard are the prettiest. But if all the leaves were scarlet, would the world be as pretty? It would be nice, but wouldn't we soon miss the contrast of colors? Scarlet leaves seem more brilliant if we see them next to gold leaves.

Many times people have a favorite tree. It may be a tree in their own yard or a tree they are privileged to see from a distance. When I was about your age my favorite tree was an old horse chestnut that grew on my block. It was a huge tree. That was one of the reasons I liked it. But it was an interesting tree too. The sidewalks under the horse chestnut were always covered with something the tree was dropping. In early spring it dropped shiny, wax-covered leaf buds. Then leaflets damaged by wind or frost began to curl and drop. During the summer the leaves always grew so close together that some were crowded off the branches and onto the walk. But what I liked most about that tree was that in the fall it dropped its leaves all at once.

I would look forward to the day when those horse-chestnut leaves would fall. I tried to be standing under the tree when that happened, and sometimes I succeeded. I would be standing on grass one minute; then as if on signal the tree would shed its leaves, and in a matter of a few moments I would be wading knee deep in them.

I believe that people are a lot like trees. They come in all shapes and sizes and colors. And all of them are needed to make up the beauty of the world. God knew what he was doing when he passed out leaves. Can you imagine a Christmas tree with palm leaves? Or can you imagine a maple tree with rubber-tree leaves? Each tree has leaves that match the rest of its structure.

And so it is with humans. We are each given talents and capabilities to match our own makeup. We never need to be jealous of what someone else has or what someone else can do, because we each have our own talents that are God-given and just right for us.

Sentence prayer: Our Father: We thank you for our special talents, as well as for our common bond of humanness. Amen.

ss It On

*er with "The birds sing sweetly in
ne" written on it.*

Þlayed the word game Pass It On?
Here's how it's played. A leader makes up a
sentence and writes it on a piece of paper. All the
players sit in a circle, and the leader whispers his
sentence to the person next to him. That person in
turn whispers the sentence to the next person, and
so on around the circle. When the sentence has
been whispered to everyone, the last person says it
out loud. The leader then reads the original
sentence from the paper. The sentence seldom
reaches the last person in the same form as it began.

For instance, here's a beginning sentence I've
used before: "The birds sing sweetly in the
springtime." By the time that sentence was passed
on to eight or ten people, its meaning had been
changed to this: "The buds swing neatly in the
springtime." The second sentence was a lot different
from the first one, wasn't it? But that's what makes
the game fun and makes the players smile.

You can also play Pass It On with deeds. Did you
ever think of that? Once I knew of a family whose
house burned down. All their possessions were lost,
but the people in the community pitched in and
helped the family out. The father of the family said,
"I don't know how I can ever repay you for what
you've done."

17

The man he was speaking to replied, "I don't want you to repay me. Not at all. When you get around to it, just pass on a good deed to someone else in need."

Now that's a good idea, isn't it? Just think of how many people do kind things for you. Your mother buys you roller skates. Your father helps you with your homework. Lots of people do kind things for you every day. Now you may not be able to return the kindness by buying roller skates for your mother or helping your dad with his homework, but you can pass on some other kindness to someone else. Maybe you can help your little brother or sister carry home a load of library books. Or maybe you could stop and visit with the old man who lives alone on your block. There are many ways in which you can pass a kindness on to another.

We learn from the Bible that God loves each of us. Surely each kind deed passed from one person to another becomes a living example of this love.

Sentence prayer: Our Father: We thank you for the many opportunities to pass kindnesses on to others. Amen.

The Magnet Within Us

Props: *Magnet, pins, paper clips.*

How many of you have ever played with a magnet? Almost all of you, I'd guess. Magnets are fun, aren't they? Did you ever wonder what a magnet really is? It's a piece of iron or steel that has the property of physically drawing certain substances to it.

When I was about your age, magnets were popular toys. Children would take them to school to play with at recess. We used to have contests to see who could lift the most pins with a magnet. Or sometimes we'd use nails. Or paper clips. I've brought some pins along today, and I'll give each of you a pin. Now, as I hold the magnet, let's see how many pins it will attract. (One at a time each child adds his pin or paper clip to the magnet.)

It's interesting to see that the pin that has been magnetized will attract another pin, and another, and another.

Did you know that people have magnets inside them? Oh, not a piece of metal like this magnet, but something different. Can any of you guess what the magnet inside of us is? If you can't guess, I'll tell you. Love is the magnet inside each of us that will attract others to us. Have you ever thought about that? If we love somebody, we may show it by smiling at him. And what happens? Right. Usually the person will smile back. And once they've smiled back, they're ready to smile at someone else. Soon we have three smiling faces.

If the love magnet within you is really working, you may do something nice for someone. For example, you might spend Saturday morning cleaning up the yard—picking up papers, toys, and other stray items—and then maybe cutting the grass. This would certainly make your parents happy, and it might even inspire them to plan a treat for you—a cookout, perhaps. The whole family can join in that fun, and don't be surprised if your next-door neighbors drop in for a hot dog or two. Don't be surprised either if the next time your neighbors make homemade ice cream they send over some for your family to taste.

The love magnet within each of us is a powerful force. And it's a force we can harness and use on a moment's notice. This week as you go about your work and play, why not use your love magnet and see how many people you can attract to you through smiles and kind deeds?

Sentence prayer: Our Father: Thank you for the love magnet within us and for your help in using it. Amen.

The Wish Stone

Prop: *A good-luck charm.*

How many of you have ever carried a good-luck charm in your pocket? Did it bring you good luck? I'm going to tell you a story about a girl who carried a wish stone in her pocket. Do you know what a wish stone is? A wish stone is a stone found in a creek bed. But it isn't just an ordinary stone. A wish stone has a hole worn in its center from the action of the water and other smaller stones. Anyone who finds such a stone is supposed to be lucky indeed; for a wish stone makes wishes come true.

Once upon a time there was a girl who found a wish stone in a creek. She put the stone in her pocket and carried it with her wherever she went. She was never afraid when she had the wish stone in her pocket, because she knew that if she got in trouble, all she had to do was wish and she'd be out of it in a flash.

One day this girl had to run an errand for her mother. She had to pass a house where there was a big German shepherd. The girl was afraid of the dog even though the dog's master usually kept the beast fenced in a pen.

But this day when the girl reached the house where the big dog lived, it was running outside the

21

fence. The dog barked and growled, and at first the girl was afraid. Then she remembered her wish stone. She thought of the wish stone and wished that the dog wouldn't bother her.

The girl walked on with sure steps just as if she weren't afraid. She called kind words to the dog. The dog barked, but it didn't chase her and it didn't bite.

When the girl returned from doing her errand, she told her mother about the dog and how her wish stone had saved her. Her mother smiled and said, "But you didn't have your wish stone with you. I found the stone in the pocket of your school dress."

"But what made the dog behave?" the girl asked.

"You did," her mother replied. "Animals can tell when people are afraid of them. But you weren't afraid."

"I would have been afraid if I'd known I didn't have my wish stone," the girl said.

"Why?" her mother asked. "You don't need a wish stone, and neither does anyone else. People make their own luck. If people remember they are created in the image of God, they know they are strong. It's a lot better to believe in yourself than to believe in a wish stone that just may not be in your pocket when you need it."

The girl knew her mother was right. She set her wish stone on her desk where it would remind her that she could be strong when she needed to be strong. With God's help she could make her own luck.

Sentence prayer: Our Father: We thank you for the courage to have faith in ourselves. Amen.

Thoughts on Ear-Wiggling

Prop: *Someone who can wiggle his/her ears (if you can't).*

Can you wiggle your ears? (Give them time to try.) I've known people who could wiggle their ears, and it always looks easy. But I can't wiggle mine. (Or, _____ can wiggle his/hers. Or, I can wiggle mine.) I do believe ear-wiggling takes a special talent.

When I was in the second grade I knew a boy named Joe who could wiggle his ears. Sometimes Joe wiggled his ears during reading class. Everyone laughed. The teacher would look up and wonder why. She couldn't see anything funny. Joe thought he had a good thing going for him. He had found a way to get lots of attention.

So Joe wiggled his ears during arithmetic class. Again everyone laughed. And again the teacher missed the joke. During spelling class Joe wiggled his ears, but this time the teacher looked up in time to see him. She laughed along with the rest of the pupils, but she suggested that Joe save his ear-wiggling for recess time.

Joe took the teacher's advice. At recess time he spent many minutes wiggling his ears. But by now his classmates were growing bored with ear-wiggling. They began to ignore Joe, and this hurt.

Now, the teacher had been watching, and she saw what was happening. Right after recess she announced that the class was going to have a talent show. She appointed Joe as chairman. It was his job to find out what the other children could do for the talent show.

Joe worked hard. He looked at his classmates with new interest. He learned that Suzie could play the piano. Jerry could yodel. Bill could blow a tune on the kazoo, and Linda could do a great imitation of a cackling hen.

The talent show was a success, and to Joe's surprise he had more fun helping the other children present their talents than he ever had wiggling his own ears. After the show Joe mentioned this to the teacher, and she smiled and said, "It's always fun to help others." And then do you know what she did? She wiggled her ears!

Sentence prayer: Our Father: We know our talents come from you. Help us to use them wisely. Amen.

Witch
of the Woods

Prop: *A picture of a witch-hazel tree.*

One November day when I was about your age I was walking through the woods and I sat down to rest for a while. I was sitting there minding my own business when—ping!—something hit me on the back of the neck. I turned around to see who was throwing things at me. But I saw nobody. I sat there a while longer and—ping! Something bounced off my left ear.

There was nobody around. I was sure of that. There wasn't even a squirrel or a bird in sight. So I came to a conclusion. That tree hated me. I ran home and told my grandfather about the tree that hated me.

Grandpa was a wise man. He didn't laugh. He said perhaps I was right. Maybe the tree did hate me, but he doubted it just a little. He walked with me back to the woods so I could point out exactly which tree it was that had it in for me, and I showed him.

"This is a witch-hazel tree." Grandpa motioned me to a limb of the tree. "Come take a look at this."

I looked and I noticed things I had missed before. Dead leaves clung stubbornly to the limbs, but there were starry blossoms among them with petals like gold threads. And among these blossoms Grandpa pointed to pods. Some of them were open, but some were closed tight. Grandpa asked me to sit beside him under the tree and listen. In a few moments we heard something ping against a nearby tree trunk.

"What was that?" I asked.

Grandpa smiled as he picked a seedpod from the witch hazel and showed it to me. The pod seemed to be made of two cells, and Grandpa explained that one of these cells could shorten like a spring and then let go to drive the seeds forth with great force. He explained that the frost and the sun decided just when the spring cell would tighten and let fly the seeds. We sat there a while longer listening to the seeds ping into the grass, and when I was satisfied that the tree didn't hate me personally, we strolled home.

"Trees are a lot like people," Grandpa said. "They do mysterious things, but once you understand them and learn what they're trying to do, you'll realize that most of them are quite interesting."

I've remembered that day and Grandpa's words a long time. Whenever I think someone has it in for me, I remember the witch-hazel tree, and I try to find out just what that person is really trying to do. Usually once I understand the person, we become friends. Whenever you think someone's picking on

27

you, I hope you'll ask yourself, "What's really going on here?" The true answer is there waiting for you to discover it.

Sentence prayer: Our Father: We thank you for the mysteries of life. Help us learn from them. Amen.

Report-Card Blues

Prop: *A report card.*

You all know what this is. It's a report card. Do you ever get the report-card blues? Some of you are smiling. Some are frowning. And I saw one boy sort of duck his head and hunch his shoulders. The sight of a report card arouses varying reactions in people.

Most children worry about their report cards. They are concerned about what their teachers think of them. They are concerned about what their parents think of them. Will a low grade mean no TV after supper? Will a low grade mean a Saturday morning study session?

Now, maybe a little less TV and a little more study would help your grades. But on the other hand maybe you've tried your best and your grades still aren't topnotch. This is discouraging. If you feel discouraged about school and grades, there's a passage in the Bible that may encourage you. In Colossians 3:23 we read, "Whatsoever ye do, work heartily, as unto the Lord, and not unto men." You may wonder what this means. It means that you should do your spelling and arithmetic and reading lessons to please God instead of your parents and teachers. In doing this you may please all three.

Did you ever ask yourself why you're going to

school? Well, the answer is to learn—to fit yourself for life. If this is the case, then school must be a part of God's plan for you. In your mind try to forget about your parents and teachers for a moment and ask yourself how you would conduct your school life in order to please God.

God is interested in you. God wants you to have the knowledge you need. God wants to see industry woven into your character. So when you start working for God and not for grades, your attitude toward school will change. Under this system your goal will be to learn, not to earn grades. But the surprise package is that if you learn, the grades will be forthcoming.

Why don't you try this idea for a quarter or a semester and see if it won't work for you? Work heartily as unto the Lord and see if a change doesn't take place in your life and on your report card.

Sentence prayer: Our Father: Help us to do our best work in all areas of our life. Amen.

Where the Action Is
(For Thanksgiving)

Prop: *A balloon.*

What would you do if I popped this balloon with a pin? Right! You'd probably jump. I'd probably jump, too, even though I wouldn't be surprised at the loud noise. If I popped this balloon and if you jumped, we'd be demonstrating a law of physics or a rule of the universe.

Sometimes young people think that they're the only ones who have rules to keep, but this isn't true. The world we live in operates under certain rules or laws. One of the rules is that there can be no action without a resultant reaction.

If I pop the balloon, that's action. When you jump, that's reaction. Now let's think about the action of being thankful. If something nice happens to us and we give thanks for it, that's action. What will the reaction be? I've found that good things come back to me in direct proportion to the thanks I've expressed.

If we're thankful for the good things we have—our homes, our parents, our health—more good things will come our way. But if we forget to be thankful for our blessings, or if we are indifferent to them, or if we criticize them, we have released a negative action. And according to the law of the

31

universe there will be a reaction. We will not be as happy as we could have been if we had been thankful.

In the Bible story of the talents, Jesus said that each man received talents according to his ability. One man received five talents; another received two talents. And a third man received one talent. Now the first two men were thankful for their talents, and they were grateful for their master's belief in their abilities and their loyalty. They began to try to increase the talents given to them.

But the third man wasn't appreciative. Instead of being thankful for one talent, he felt cheated. He thought his master unfair, so he hid his talent. And the law of the universe worked for all three men. The two who were thankful for what had been given to them increased their talents. The man who criticized his gift lost the one he had.

This year at Thanksgiving let's all be sure to give thanks for the many blessings we have received. And let's carry our Thanksgiving spirit into the rest of the year. If you do this, you'll find that your action of giving thanks will result in a reaction of happiness. So let's give thanks, not to be good, but to be happy.

Sentence prayer: Our Father: We thank you for all our many blessings so freely given. Amen.

32

Who Is God?

Prop: *A blank sheet of drawing paper.*

If you have attended church or Sunday school very many times, you've probably heard quite a bit about God. Many of you are probably wondering who God is. This is as close as we can get to a picture of God. (Show prop.) You can't see God. Yet there is much evidence that God is there. If you say, "Who is God?" my answer will be, "God is love. God is the spirit of love."

I want each of you to think about your parents for a moment. At bedtime they come into your room with you. After you're tucked in for the night, they turn out the light. Now the room is dark. But you know your parents are still there. Just because you can't see them doesn't mean that they're gone. That's the way it is with God. God is near even though you can't see him.

What tells you that your parents love you? They do things for you, don't they? Just think of all the things they do for you. They provide a neat house for you to live in. They provide suitable clothes for you to wear. They provide good food for you to eat. All these things tell you that your parents love you.

So it is with God. God has given you the world to live in. All the beautiful things you see each day come from God: the flowers, the birds, the sunrise, the sunset, the mountains, the forests, the ocean, the rivers and streams. All these wonders came from God for you to enjoy. They tell you that God loves you.

You may ask, "How can God love so many people at the same time?" Think again about your parents. Your parents love each other, although they may be separated during the day. They love your grandparents, who may live in another city or another state. They love your aunts and uncles, who may also live far from you. They love you at home at the same time they love your brothers and sisters at different schools. Love knows no boundaries.

Whenever you feel like asking, "Who is god?" think about this answer. (Write "LOVE" on prop. Show it.) God is love.

Sentence prayer: Our Father: We thank you for the many blessings that demonstrate your love for us. Amen.

Silent Night, Holy Night
(For Christmas)

Prop: *Hymnal open to "Silent Night, Holy Night."*

All of us know the Christmas hymn "Silent Night, Holy Night" (show prop), but I wonder how many of us have ever stopped to think who wrote the words and who wrote the music. This famous Christmas carol was written on December 24 in the year 1818—over one hundred fifty years ago. Did you have any idea that "Silent Night, Holy Night" was that old?

In the little village of Obendorf in Bavaria, the parish priest, Father Joseph Mohr, wrote a poem in honor of Christmas Eve. To Father Mohr, Christmas Eve was the most holy night of the year. He gave the poem to Franz Gruber, the church organist, asking if Mr. Gruber could set the words to music.

Franz Gruber was inspired by the simplicity of the poem, and he composed a melody for it in just a few hours' time. The two men, Father Mohr and the organist Franz Gruber, decided to use the new hymn in the Christmas Eve mass that night. Can't you just imagine how proud and eager they were to share their work with the village worshipers? But the worship service failed to come off exactly as planned. Father Mohr and organist Gruber discov-

35

ered at the last minute that the organ wasn't working as it should. They would be unable to use it in their Christmas Eve service. But they didn't give up their idea of sharing "Silent Night, Holy Night" with the villagers.

The parish people heard the new hymn for the first time sung as a duet and accompanied by guitar. Perhaps some of you thought the guitar was a new thing in church services. Not so. Here we have a record of guitar accompaniment being used over one hundred and fifty years ago. That night at mass Father Mohr sang the tenor lead, and Franz Gruber sang bass and played the guitar.

This was not a very showy beginning for a hymn that was to become the foremost Christmas carol of the world. Perhaps its humble beginning matched the humble surroundings at the birth of Christ. And perhaps there is a lesson for us in the history of this hymn, the lesson that pomp and circumstance and great show do not necessarily make great events. Things of lasting value often spring from humble sources.

Sentence prayer: Our Father: Thank you for showing us through the Christ Child that humble beginnings may precede true greatness. Amen.

Angels
(For Christmas)

Props: *A guarantee card and a halo.*

Do you know what this card is? It's a guarantee. A guarantee is a promise that something will work as it is advertised to work. Most people hesitate to buy anything these days unless it carries a guarantee card.

The Christmas season is the time when we hear a lot about angels. Do you recognize this? Yes, it's a halo. It represents the glow of light that supposedly surrounds an angel's head. Not many of us have had the opportunity to see an angel. We see pictures of what artists think angels look like. We see actors in Christmas plays dressed the way play directors believe angels must have dressed. Few of us have actually seen an angel.

Yet the Bible guarantees us angels. Oh, we don't actually get a card that says, "One angel guaranteed," but in the book of Psalms we read, "For he shall give his angels charge over thee, to keep thee in all thy ways." We have this guarantee. The Bible guarantees us angels. But where are they?

The early Hebrews pictured angels as a group of heavenly creatures surrounding God and bringing guidance and goodwill to people for whom God had a special message. Scholars have found that most words come from another word in a language—a root word. They also have learned that the Hebrew word from which *angel* comes means nothing more than "messenger."

We may agree that an angel is a messenger from God, but we have never seen such a messenger. Surely God is still sending messages. If so, where are all the creatures with the filmy wings and the white robes and the golden halos?

I'll tell you what I believe. I believe that God sends angels to us in the form of good thoughts. If you try thinking of angels as good thoughts, can't you remember knowing some angels? What about the thought that told you to smile at your teacher this morning? What about the thought that told you to help your mother yesterday? Didn't that thought make your day a little bit happier? And sometimes when you have a problem in your life, doesn't a thought come to you that will help solve that problem in a good way?

I believe that angels are all around us. The Bible guarantees them. But like all guarantees, the guarantee of angels also carries a responsibility. If you buy a new watch, it's only guaranteed to work if you take good care of it. The manufacturer won't honor its guarantee if you take the watch apart to see what makes it tick, or if you let it go through the washer in the pocket of your favorite jeans.

So, if we want to know angels, we must take the responsibility of keeping our minds open to the messages God sends to us. We mustn't let our minds become clogged with unloving or selfish thoughts. During this Christmas season while you're thinking about Santa and Christmas trees, I hope you'll think about Christmas angels—and listen for their messages.

Sentence prayer: Our Father: We thank you for the guarantee of angels and for your help in recognizing them. Amen.

The Nicest Gift
(For Christmas)

Prop: *Cardboard box, gift wrapped for Christmas.*

It's the time of year when we're all interested in Christmas presents. We're interested in the ones we'll give, as well as the ones we'll receive. Sometimes giving gifts can be a real problem. You may know exactly what your brothers and sisters want, but you may not have enough money to buy it. Or you may have money saved to buy your parents a present, but you're stuck for a gift idea.

Did you ever wonder what the nicest gift in the world might be? A doll? A sled? A bicycle? Yes. Those are all nice gifts. And they're all gifts you can buy. But there's one gift that money can't buy, and it's a gift that everyone wants. People seldom mention wanting this gift. Perhaps they don't even realize they need it. But the thing that everyone wants is to feel that he counts in the scheme of life.

Everyone has moments when he feels that he doesn't count for very much. Perhaps you feel this way sometimes at school. Maybe Suzie is the best speller, and Danny is the best reader; Joe is fast at numbers, and Jan always gets first place in the lunch line. Where do you fit in?

Do you ever remember feeling that nobody cared much about you? Then maybe your teacher thumbtacked *your* picture onto the bulletin board where everyone could see it. Remember how good you felt then? Suddenly you were important; you counted for something. Your teacher gave you one of the nicest gifts in the world.

Everyone needs to feel special once in a while. And making people feel special is a gift you can give to everyone you know. You may not be able to wrap it up in a box and tie it with a bow. And you may not be able to tack it to a bulletin board. But that won't matter.

Along with your boxed gift to your grandmother you might ask her advice on something. This would make her feel important. Or you might ask her to help you make her special cookies for Christmas dinner. You might ask your uncle to tell you about his best Christmas.

It might be a good idea if each of us would think about making those we care about feel special. It could be one of the nicest gifts of Christmastime. It could be a gift that lasts all year.

Sentence prayer: Our Father: Help us recognize with words and deeds the specialness of those around us. Amen.

Living Is Sharing
(For Christmas)

Prop: *Cardboard box, gift wrapped for Christmas.*

We all look forward to giving and receiving gifts during the Christmas season. But have you ever stopped to think about what all this gift-exchanging really means? When we give a gift, we're expressing our feelings of love toward another person. We're confirming the ties that bind us to other people. And we're expressing a basic desire to be united with others through love.

But the Christmas gifts we exchange with friends and family have a deeper meaning. They're symbols of universal sharing. They're a reminder that sharing is a basic necessity for all forms of life.

Did you ever stop to think that no living creature can make it in this world strictly on his own? That is a fact of nature. All the plants that grow in our world share space and sunshine. They share rainfall. They share the soil. The same thing is true of animals and humans. Nobody has a lease on the sun or on the rain clouds or on the nutrients in the earth.

Hundreds of years ago men and women lived by hunting and by gathering wild plants. It made good sense to share with each other. As the world progressed, some kinds of sharing came to be the subject of laws. The law of Moses forbade persons

42

from harvesting all corners of their fields. They were to leave some for the poor.

In our lives today many of us do not raise crops. We depend on others to do this for us; then we buy what we need. But the need to share is still with us. Two-thirds of the world's people go to bed hungry. We may not be able to actually give a bushel of wheat to some needy person, but we can share what we have.

The pennies or nickles or dimes that we are willing to give to the less fortunate count for good. All of our Christmas gifts—whether to family and friends, to strangers in foreign lands, or to the unfortunate in this country—are indications of the need for universal sharing. Let us remember that our personal contributions to the hungry of the world are valued more than we may ever know. Let us remember that to live is to share.

Sentence prayer: Our Father: We thank thee for thy bountiful goodness and for the need to share with others. Amen.

The Wish List

Prop: *A long list on a long streamer of paper.*

You may be wondering what this long paper is. I'll tell you. It's a list of all the nice things I wish other people would do for me. You might call it a wish list. Have you ever made out a wish list? Maybe you haven't written one down on paper, but you've probably thought about things you wish other people would do for you. I think every one of us has a wish list tucked away somewhere in his mind.

Would you like to hear some of my wish list? First, I often wish people would smile at me. Now that's pretty simple, isn't it? It doesn't take much effort to smile. And number two on this list is praise. I often wish people would notice the nice things I do and praise me for doing them. Do you ever feel that way? Maybe you've gone to a lot of trouble to make your bed very neatly. Don't you like it when someone notices and comments on it? Sure! Everyone likes praise.

Another thing on my list is that I wish people would be friendly and include me in their plans. Almost everyone wants a friend. Now that's just three things on this long list, and I'm sure that if each of you made out a wish list you'd have a lot of different things on it.

44

THE WISH LIST

How many of you know the golden rule? Right. Do unto others as you would have them do unto you. I got to thinking about that rule when I finished my wish list, and do you know what I'm going to try to do? I'm going to try to do all these wish-list things to other people. If this is what I want folks to do to me, I should be willing to do these same things to them. Wouldn't that make the world a happy place? Just think!

Everybody would be smiling at everyone else. Everyone would be praising his neighbor's good deeds. Everyone would be friendly. If everyone followed the golden rule, war would stop. Did you realize that you can stop wars? Maybe you can't stop wars between nations, but by using the golden rule you can stop the small wars that threaten to start up around you at home, at school, and on the playground. All you have to remember is the golden rule.

I'm going to put my wish list in my pocket, but I'm not going to forget about it. And every time I think of it I'm going to think of doing my wish deeds to others. Why don't you try doing that this week and just see what happens?

Sentence prayer: Our Father: We thank you for the golden rule and for your help in using it. Amen.

The Salt of the Earth

Prop: *A saltshaker.*

You may be wondering why I've brought a saltshaker here today. The Bible says, "Ye are the salt of the earth." Did you ever think about that? Do you know what it means? I'm going to tell you a once-upon-a-time story that may help you understand.

Once upon a time there was a man who thought a lot. Sometimes he sat around all day just thinking. He was trying to decide what was the most important thing in the world. Sometimes he asked people this question and received a lot of different answers.

Some people said money was the most important thing in the world because without it a person had nothing and with it a person could have anything he wanted. But the thinker knew this wasn't true. Sometimes people who were very sick couldn't buy health for any amount of money.

Another person said health was the most important thing in the world. But the thinker knew that some very sick people had done some very great things with their lives; so that answer didn't satisfy him either. Love? Honesty? Truth? The man considered all these answers, but they didn't satisfy him. At last he decided that he must be asking the wrong people. Children were known for speaking the truth; so the man stopped a girl who was walking with her mother. "What do you think is the most important thing in the world?" he asked.

The girl thought for a few moments; then she said, "I am."

The man was surprised, and the girl's mother was shocked. "How unseemly to think so well of yourself," the mother said to her daughter.

The thinker just smiled and walked on; then he stopped a boy who was playing ball in the park. "Son, what do you think is the most important thing in the world?"

The boy stopped to think. At last he said, "I am. I'm the most important thing in the world." Now the boy's friends heard this, and they began to laugh.

"Wow! Is he ever conceited!" one boy shouted.

"Swellhead," shouted another.

The boy blushed in embarrassment, but the thinker came to his rescue. He called all the boys to him and said, "Your friend is right. He is the most important thing in the world. I've talked to many people, and now I see that this is the best answer."

"What makes you think you're so important?" one boy asked his friend.

"Because I think I'm important, I know the things I do are important. So I'm really careful to try to do what's right."

"Humph!" the second boy snorted. "So maybe *I*

think *I'm* the most important thing in the world.
Then what? Everybody can't be the most important
thing in the world."

The thinker didn't want to hear friends in
argument, so he spoke up. "You, too, are the most
important thing in the world. *People* are the most
important thing in the world—all people. And the
better people think of themselves and the more they
try to do what's right and best for the world, the
better place we'll all have to live in."

That's the end of the story. When you sit down at
home to eat a meal, what is always on the table?
The saltshaker, isn't it? It's not the biggest thing on
the table, but the meal would taste flat without what
it contains, wouldn't it? God was paying man quite a
compliment when he said, "Ye are the salt of the
earth." He was saying that people are the most
important things in the world. They are basic.
Without them, the world would be dull and
uninteresting. Ye are the salt of the earth.

Sentence prayer: Our Father: We thank you that
we are the salt of the earth, and
we know you will help us
always to try to do what is good
and right in your sight. Amen.

48

What's New to You?

Prop: *Ask a child from another church to visit.*

Have you ever been the new person in a group?
_____ is new to this group. (Introduce
visiting child.) It's sort of a scary feeling, isn't it,
_____? As _____ can tell you, it's a little hard
to step into a group when you don't know the rest of
the people. You don't know what they like. You
don't know what they'll think of you. It's an uneasy
situation.

I want to tell you a funny story about what
happened to me when my family moved to a new
town and I had to attend a new school. There I was
in a classroom of strangers, but I could spot the
leader of the ingroup. You know how that goes.
You can usually spot the person who seems to lead
the others. In this school that leader happened to be
a boy, and he happened to be the editor of the
school paper published every month.

Now I really admired this boy, but I didn't know
how to go about making friends with him. I heard he
was interested in tropical fish, so I approached him
on that subject. I mentioned to him that my
aquarium glass was covered with a green scum that I
couldn't get rid of. The boy didn't say much at the
time, and I really felt snubbed.

But a couple days later this boy dropped a magazine clipping on my desk. He said nothing, just dropped the clipping. I read it, and to my surprise I found it was an article giving rules for writing essays. At first I was puzzled, then I remembered that the boy was editor of the school paper. I grew excited. Surely this clipping meant that he wanted me to write something for the paper.

That afternoon after school I wrote an essay about tropical fish. Writing an essay was a new experience. I erased and I rewrote. I tore up one copy and started over. But at last I finished the essay and gave it to the editor. Then I worried all day about what he would think of my writing.

It wasn't until after lunch that the teacher called me and the other boy to her desk and thanked me for writing the essay. She said it would be used in the next issue of the paper. I in turn thanked the editor for giving me the clipping containing the rules for writing essays. To my surprise the boy looked puzzled.

"I didn't give you any clipping on writing," he said.

I reached into my pocket where I'd kept the clipping. I pulled it out and showed it to him. He smiled. Then he turned the clipping over and pointed to another article. This article told how to get rid of aquarium algae. We both had a good laugh over the mix-up.

50

"How lucky that you read the wrong side of the clipping," the boy said.

The teacher smiled. "How lucky that you had the courage to try something new."

I've always remembered this incident, and I've always remembered that teacher's words. "How lucky that you had the courage to try something new." I hope you'll remember those words. They could change your life.

Sentence prayer: Our Father: Thank you for the courage to face all situations. Amen.

The Hole
in the Net

Prop: *Fish net with a hole.*

How many of you have aquariums or fishbowls? Fish make nice pets, but there always comes that day when their home has to be cleaned. Like all living creatures, a fish needs a clean place to live.

The other day I was cleaning out an aquarium, and I was having a hard time catching the fish. When I took a closer look at my net I discovered that it had a hole in it. The hole wasn't big, but it was big enough to let the fish escape.

Now the fish didn't know what I was trying to do. When they felt themselves surrounded by the net they sensed trouble. They darted this way and that for a moment or two, but each time they would find the hole and escape from their trouble.

I finally gave up catching any fish with that net. I went to the family sewing basket, got a needle and thread, and mended the hole. Now I'm not very good at threading a needle, and while I was trying to get that thread through the needle eye, I had lots of time to think.

As I thought, I realized that sometimes people aren't as smart as fish. When trouble surrounded the fish, they swam for the escape hole. But what do people do when they're in trouble? They have an escape hole too, but sometimes they forget to use it. Do you know what man's escape hole is?

Prayer is man's escape hole. When we can't solve our troubles alone, we can always turn to God in prayer. But instead of heading for the escape hole, people will worry a lot. Sometimes they worry until they can't eat or sleep. Or they may act foolishly and say things they're sorry for later.

Prayers needn't and shouldn't be a listing of troubles. God knows what your troubles are. You may say that you're too young to pray. But that isn't true. A prayer can be quite simple, as simple as: "Thy will be done. Thank you." Or: "God is with me. I give thanks."

The next time you feel surrounded by trouble, be as smart as a fish. Go right to the escape hole. Pray.

Sentence prayer: Our Father: We thank you that you are ever-present. Amen.

Thoughts on Mirrors

Prop: *A mirror.*

You've all seen mirrors. Of course! They're made from glass and some silvery stuff, and when you look into one you can see yourself. But do you like what you see?

A leading doctor has learned that most people dislike what they see in their mirrors. They're sure other people look just fine, but when *they* look into the mirror all they can see are ears sticking out or eyes too far apart or a nose that can look like a banana.

When I was younger I looked into a few mirrors, and every time I did I saw a scrawny kid that the other boys nicknamed Skinny. One day my grandmother caught me looking into a mirror and said, "What do you see?"

"I see a scrawny kid too little to be good for anything."

Grandmother studied me carefully. "That's not what I see. I see a boy who's going to grow tall if he just gives himself a little time."

"But what am I supposed to do while I'm

54

waiting?" I asked. "You know growing takes forever."

"If I were you," Grandmother said, "I'd look into that mirror until I saw something about myself that I liked. It doesn't have to be a big thing. Just find some little thing that you really like about yourself. Then if I were you, I'd remember that thing. Whenever anybody called me Skinny, I'd pay no attention. I'd just remember the good thing about myself."

I tried to follow this advice. I looked at my mouth—too big. I looked at my nose—like a ski slope. Then I noticed something. On my left cheek I had a freckle that was shaped exactly like a star. Right then I decided that freckle was the thing about me that I liked. I had a perfect star of a freckle.

And this was my secret. I didn't tell a soul, but when kids called me Skinny, I just grinned and remembered my star freckle. As I grew older I outgrew my need for that freckle. I realized that my mouth and nose weren't really any worse looking than anyone else's.

The Bible tells us to love our neighbor as ourself. Unless we love ourselves we can't really love our neighbor, can we? We have to accept ourselves before we can accept the person next to us or across the world from us. Once you've found something to like about yourself, then you're ready to look at another person and find what you like about her.

Why don't you experiment this week? Look into a mirror and see what good things you can see.

Sentence prayer: Our Father: Help us love ourselves and our neighbors, knowing we are all created in your image. Amen.

Captain Cook, Peacemaker

Prop: *A can of sauerkraut.*

How many of you like sauerkraut? How many of you have ever tasted it? Some people think it makes a mighty good meal. The Bible has a group of verses called the Beatitudes, and one of those verses begins "Blessed are the peacemakers." Now, you're probably wondering what sauerkraut has to do with peacemakers, but I have a story to share with you that will explain it.

Once there was a man named Captain Cook. He was a famous explorer who sailed the seas discovering new lands. Captain Cook had a serious problem. His sailors kept getting sick. In those days doctors knew that sailors sometimes got a disease called scurvy when they didn't get enough vitamin C, the vitamin found in oranges and grapefruit and cabbage.

Sometimes Captain Cook was at sea for months at a time. He couldn't carry enough citrus fruit and cabbage to last the trip. Then he had an idea.

Sauerkraut was made from cabbage, and it could be stored for a long time.

On his next voyage Captain Cook brought along barrels of sauerkraut. His sailors hated it. They threatened mutiny. But Captain Cook had another idea. He asked his ship's officers to pretend that they liked the sauerkraut. Then he served no more of it to the sailors. Only the officers found sauerkraut on their plates. The officers pretended to like it. In fact, they pretended until they really did like it.

At last the sailors began to complain. They felt they were being slighted; maybe there was something about the sauerkraut they hadn't noticed at first taste. They demanded sauerkraut. Weren't they as important as the officers?

Captain Cook must have smiled a bit to himself as he saw the sailors gobbling the sauerkraut, but his problems were solved. His sailors were happy, as well as healthy.

Captain Cook was a peacemaker. He could have ordered his men to eat the sauerkraut and risked having a mutiny on his hands, but he was smart. He thought of a way to make his men want to obey. I think we can learn from Captain Cook. It's important for all of us to be peacemakers. If your sister or brother grabs the toy you want, or if you and your friend get into an argument, remember Captain Cook and the sauerkraut. See if you can find a peaceful answer to the problem. Peace starts with you and with me. It starts right in our families, right in our own living rooms. Blessed are the peacemakers.

Sentence prayer: Our Father: Thank you for our daily opportunities to make peace, and help us to find the peaceful way of living our lives. Amen.

Sandpaper or Velvet?

Props: *Squares of sandpaper and squares of velvet.*

Once upon a time there was a man who tried an experiment. He cut out several squares of sandpaper like these; then he cut out several squares of velvet like these. Which one of these squares do you like the best? The one that feels rough and scratchy or the one that feels soft and smooth?

This man walked down the street in his hometown and asked everyone he met, "How are you today?" If the person said, "I am not feeling well," or if he said, "I am sick of this terrible weather," or if he said, "I am afraid I may be catching a cold," the man gave that person a square of sandpaper. But if the person said, "I am feeling great" or "I am enjoying this gentle rain," or if the person said, "I am just fine," the man gave him a square of velvet.

Now these people didn't know what to think. The ones who received sandpaper dropped it in the nearest trash can. But the ones who received velvet kept it. They stuck the velvet in their pockets or their purses.

Finally a man who had been listening to all this

asked the man what he was doing. He said, "Oh, it's just a game. When I ask someone how he is and he gives me a happy answer, I give him a square of velvet to help remind him of what a pleasant place the world is. I give sandpaper to the people who take the Lord's name in vain. The sandpaper is to remind them of how rough they're making things for themselves."

"But I didn't hear anyone take the Lord's name in vain," the friend said.

"They didn't realize they did it," the man said. "But they did take the Lord's name in vain. When Moses asked God his name, God replied, 'I am that I am.' And he told Moses that I AM was his name for ever unto all generations. Since God is supreme and perfect, he cannot be sick. God cannot be tired. God cannot be worried. So when a person says, 'I am tired' or 'I am sick,' he is taking God's name in vain."

When the people learned why this man was giving out sandpaper and velvet, they were more careful with their words. In fact they were so careful that the man didn't need any more sandpaper; soon the whole town was carrying velvet. And the more often the people said, "I am fine," "I am happy," or "I am pleased," the more often their words became true. It was almost as if their words were seeds. Their good words sprouted into happenings.

Whenever anyone asks you how you are, I hope

you'll think twice before you answer. Ask yourself, "Do I want sandpaper or velvet?"

Sentence prayer: Our Father: We thank you that we are created in your image. Help us strive for your perfection. Amen.

Forth
Hand

Pr *ose of the children.*

Today I want you to do something for me. I want you to stretch out your hand to the person next to you. Go on. Right now. Join hands with your neighbor.

All right. Now that you've joined hands you may let go. Do you know what happened when you were holding hands? Everyone of you smiled at your neighbor. It was so automatic you probably didn't even know you were doing it. But you smiled.

When Jesus healed the withered hand of the man in the synagogue he commanded, "Stretch forth thy hand!" When the man obeyed the command his hand was made whole again. A miracle! No doubt this man with the withered hand had been to doctors who had failed to cure him. But when he stretched out his hand to Christ, his hand was made whole.

Stretch forth thy hand. It seems to me that those four words will never go out of style. They radiate the spirit of Christianity. Think what a wonderful place the world would be if everyone stretched out his hand to others in friendship. Think what miracles might happen if bosses stretched out a hand of friendship to the people who worked for them. And

63

what might happen if each race on this earth stretched out a hand of friendship to every other race.

When nations, religions, races, stretch out their hands in friendship, wars will stop and the world will be at peace. You may wonder how all this concerns you. But it does concern you. The peace of the world rests with each individual. We have to have friendship in the family before we can have friendship in the community. We must have friendship in the community before we can have friendship in the nation. And we must have friendship within each nation before we can have friendship in the world.

All this friendship begins with the individual—with you and with me. So don't wait for the other person to step forward and offer you his hand. *You* start it. To have a friend, be a friend. Stretch forth thy hand.

Sentence prayer: Our Father: Be with us as we stretch forth our hands to others in friendship. Amen.

The Green-Eyed Monster

Prop: *A green or green-eyed monster.*

Do you know what this ugly creature is? It's jealousy, the green-eyed monster. Sometimes when we're not careful this monster will try to come live inside us. Now of course he can't really get inside us, but his ideas might get into our heads and make us unhappy.

Sometimes it's hard to tell if this green-eyed monster's ideas are getting into your mind. This fellow is sneaky. But have you ever thought that your brother or sister was getting more attention from your parents than you were getting? And have you thought, "Hmmm, I'll have to get even with them."

I think we've all had ideas like that at times, and that's one example of the green-eyed monster working. Maybe you thought your brother got a bigger piece of pie than you did. So you decided to even the score by snitching half of the candy bar he had hidden under his pillow. And what happened? A row. And maybe you got a stomachache from too many sweets. It was all the fault of the green-eyed monster.

What can we do about this fellow? Is there any way we can stop his dirty work? Of course there are ways to stop jealousy. It's really silly to be unhappy when something good comes to someone besides ourselves. When good comes to someone else, we really should give thanks. Now you may say, "So my brother gets to stay up a half hour later than I do! For this I should be thankful!"

And I say, "Yes, you should." Be happy for your brother and his extra half hour. Doesn't it tell you something? Doesn't it tell you that staying up an extra half hour is possible? If your brother can gain that privilege, so can you. You may have to grow up a little. But staying up an extra half hour is possible. Give thanks instead of being unhappy.

If we all turn into grouches when we see someone else get something we thought we should have, do you know what's going to happen? You can guess. Nobody likes a grouch. If we're grouchy and sullen, people will avoid us and associate with someone who's smiling and pleasant. When we're grouchy we cut down on our power to be happy. And for every minute we're grouchy we lose sixty seconds of happiness.

A sure way to keep the green-eyed monster out of our lives is to make friends with success by giving thanks for it wherever we see it no matter who has it.

If we keep smiling—and if we keep trying—the next success may be our own.

Sentence prayer: Our Father: We give thanks for our present success and for the knowledge that all things are possible through God. Amen.

Dead-End Street

Prop: *A DEAD END street sign or a drawing of one.*

How many of you have ever seen a sign like this one? Do you know what it means? A dead-end street is one that doesn't join other streets. Have you ever turned onto a dead-end street by mistake? The first thing you learned was that you could go no farther. You had to turn around or back out. Most people avoid dead-end streets.

Teachers tell me that most of their pupils worry about making friends. Many children sometimes feel that the other children don't like them. I've been thinking that over. Probably everyone has felt that way at some time or other. I know I have. Some days I feel as if nobody really cares to be around me. When I ask myself why this is, I come up with the thought that maybe I'm acting like a dead-end street.

I'll try to explain. Have you ever gone up to a classmate and said something like, "I'm sleepy this morning because I stayed up late watching TV last night." Or maybe you've said, "I'm tired of eating school lunch, so I brought my own lunch today."

Whether you realize it or not, these statements are like dead-end signs. They lead nowhere. What do you expect your classmate to say? About the TV watching he might say, "You did?" And about the home lunch he might say, "Did you?" And after that you've reached a dead end.

How do you think this other person feels? You probably made him feel unimportant because your talk was centered on you and not on him. We all like to feel important. You'll have more friends if you'll throw away the dead-end signs in your talk and make your conversation a *through* street.

Sometimes you can do this by asking questions instead of making statements. You might ask, "Did you watch TV last night?" This gives the other person a chance to tell you something about himself. Then you might add that you're sleepy from being up late and ask him if he feels that way too.

When you make another person feel that you're interested in him, then he'll like you and be interested in you. That's the way life is when you travel on the through streets.

This week I want you to remember this dead-end sign. Whenever you feel left out of things, ask yourself if your talk has accidentally turned onto a dead-end street. If the answer is yes, then turn your talk around or start all over; but get your

conversation back on the through street to friendship.

Sentence prayer: Our Father: Keep us on the
through streets of life. Amen.

Be Ye Kind

Props: *A sign bearing the words "Be Ye Kind" and cards for each of the children bearing the same message.*

When I was a child attending Sunday school, my mother would always ask, "What Bible verse did you learn today?" For several weeks in a row I replied that the Bible verse was "Be ye kind." The second week Mother said, "Again?" And the third week she said, "Are you sure that was the verse for today?" After I assured her that it was, she smiled and said, "Well, it's one of the most important thoughts we can have. I guess that's why your teacher has chosen it for so many weeks."

Mother was right. *Be ye kind.* Those are three very important words. They can change your whole life.

Do you ever fuss with your brother or sister? You do? And do you feel sorry afterward? Most of us feel sorry when we've quarreled with somebody we love. So what do you do about it? Do you promise yourself that you won't fuss again? That's what most of us do. We really want to be better people in the future than we have been in the past. But what happens to those promises?

What do you do the next time your little sister breaks your favorite crayons, the crayons that were on your own desk and strictly out of bounds for her?

As you look at your broken crayons you may forget your promise not to fuss with your sister. You may give her a clout and shower her with angry words. She'll probably respond in kind, and before you know it you'll have a real fuss going. And after it's all over, you'll feel sorry. You'll know that hitting and shouting got you nowhere. How can you prevent this from happening time and time again?

Maybe I can help you help yourself. I've written three words on each of these cards, and I'm going to give a card to each of you. You've probably already guessed that the words are "Be ye kind." I want you to put the card where you'll see it every day. Lay it on your desk. Or stick it in the corner of your mirror. And the next time you feel angry at someone, look at this card before you start a fuss. You may not be able to change your feelings, but you can change your actions if you really try. Be ye kind. Keep your card in your sight and in your memory. Prove by your actions that you know what these words mean. Why not try this plan and see if life doesn't become more pleasant at your house.

Sentence prayer: Our Father: Help us to treat every person we meet with kindness. Amen.

Love Thy Neighbor

Prop: *A sign that says, "Love Your Neighbor."*

We all know that the Bible tells us to love our neighbor. (Show prop.) But sometimes that's hard to do. We have so many neighbors. A neighbor can be someone who lives in the same neighborhood as we do. Or a neighbor can be someone we know at school or Sunday school. Or a neighbor can be a person in another part of the city, in another part of the state, or even in another part of the world. Everyone has lots of neighbors. But for right now we're going to think about your neighbors in your classroom at school or Sunday school.

It's easy to love the neighbors who are nice and quiet and well mannered. But what about the show-off neighbor. Or what about the neighbor who crowds into the lunch line out of turn? Or what about the neighbor who tattles?

You may wonder how you're supposed to love someone when you don't like the things this person does. Maybe loving means trying to understand a person. Have you ever asked yourself why a certain boy shows off? Does he get little attention at home? Or is he such a failure in certain areas at school that he feels a need to show off to get attention in other areas?

And what about the lunch-line crowder? Why does she feel such a need to be first? Maybe she feels left out of things. And have you ever tried to understand a person who tattles? Maybe it's his only way of gaining the attention he craves.

Trying to understand a person's unbecoming behavior is certainly one way of loving that person. It's hard to dislike someone you understand. Once you understand why a neighbor behaves as he does, the next step in loving him may be to be concerned about him, to help him become the best person he can become.

Ask the show-off to tell you about his dog. Once he knows someone is interested in him, he may feel less need to show off. Try helping the line crowder by asking her to sit with your gang at lunch. Maybe being included in a group of friends will seem a greater reward than being first in line. And the person who tattles may change his ways if you give him some extra attention.

It's true that you may never like certain people, but if you try to understand them, if you are concerned enough to try to help them, you have loved them.

Sentence prayer: Our Father: Help us to express loving concern for all our neighbors. Amen.

Give God
Equal Time

Prop: *A yardstick or ruler you can break in half.*

Do you all know what *equal* means? (Show prop.) If I break this in the middle (break ruler), I'll get two equal parts. Each one is the same length as the other. That's equal.

We hear a lot these days about equal time. Have you noticed that? For instance, if one political candidate airs his views on TV for thirty minutes, we can almost be sure that within a short time his opponent will demand equal time to present his views. In general this is a good thing. To be well informed we need to hear and understand both sides of a question.

You probably expect equal time at home, don't you? Suppose you and your brother are playing ball and a window is broken. Who gets to explain to your parents? Are you content to let your brother tell all the whys and wherefores? Probably not. You may let him have his say first, but it's only natural for you to want equal time to present your side of the story.

Giving the other person equal time is usually the fair way to act, and if it works between humans, it should also work between humans and God. Are you giving God equal time?

75

What is prayer? Some people say that prayer is talking to God. In a way this is right, but I like to think of prayer in broader terms. I believe that prayer is a conversation with God. Are you thinking, "What's the difference?" Well, there's a lot of difference. When you talk to God, you're implying that God is doing all the listening. But if you consider prayer as a conversation with God, then you're going to have to do some listening as well as talking. Had you ever thought of that?

During your prayer time have you ever listened for God to talk to you? Now I don't mean that you'll actually hear spoken words from God. But if you listen, his message may come to you in the form of thoughts. After you've said something to God in prayer, pause for a moment and see what thoughts flow into your mind. Perhaps these thoughts are God's reply. But you may wonder how you can be sure that the thoughts are replies from God.

It's fairly easy to know. If your thoughts are loving, kind, unselfish, then it's safe to believe that they came from God. The important thing to remember is that we should not spend all our prayer time talking. Spend part of it listening. Give God equal time.

Sentence prayer: Our Father: We thank you for the knowledge that we can have a prayer conversation with you. Amen.

Tale of
a Grapefruit

Prop: *A grapefruit.*

As you grow up you'll hear a lot about universal truths. A universal truth is a rule that holds true for all time and for all people. Rules, you say. Just more rules to learn! But obeying universal rules makes our lives more pleasant.

For instance, you've all learned the universal rule that if you touch fire you'll be burned. You learn at an early age to avoid touching fire. The rule makes your life more pleasant. And you know that the kind of seed you sow determines the kind of crop you'll reap. And from this truth we have a spin-off truth; seeking revenge is a useless waste of time and energy.

What is revenge? If someone hits you and you try to get even by hitting back, that's revenge. Revenge means getting even. Some people spend a lot of time thinking up different ways of revenge. I know of a boy who thought one of his classmates was spreading untrue stories about him at school. This boy wanted revenge; so he spent his study period thinking up stories to spread about his enemy. He was so busy thinking up mean stories that he didn't study his spelling words and he flunked his spelling test. Revenge never pays off.

The person who hits others or spreads untrue stories about others is sowing a certain kind of seed, isn't he? And what he sows, he will reap. You don't have to worry at all about putting him in his place. His own deeds will do that. A person who specializes in hitting others or telling tales will soon become very unpopular with his classmates. He'll reap unpopularity from his deeds, and if he's smart he'll change his ways.

We'll all do ourselves a favor if we forget about getting even. I once heard a story about a girl who was walking down the street minding her own business when the town bully threw a grapefruit at her. Her first reaction was to get even by flinging the grapefruit back at the bully. But then she had second thoughts. She took the grapefruit home and made grapefruit juice which she enjoyed. Then she took the grapefruit seeds and planted them in the garden. That fall the girl had five pretty house plants to share with her friends.

And what happened to the bully? The girl had been so busy and so happy taking care of her grapefruit plants that she forgot all about him.

When you leave church this morning nobody is going to throw a grapefruit at you. But during the week if something unfair happens to you, think about the girl and the grapefruit before you decide to seek revenge.

Sentence prayer: Our Father: Thank you for the universal laws that enrich our lives and leave us free to do thy will. Amen.

The Kite

Prop: *A piece of string, perhaps long enough that one child can hold one end, and another child, the other end.*

You're probably thinking—"Well, that's one long piece of string." And you're right. It is a long piece of string. Once upon a time there was a kite on one end of this string. And on the other end, there was a little girl.

Now this girl said, "Daddy, may I go fly my kite?"

Daddy said, "Yes. But don't go to the park. There are too many trees there. Your kite will get snagged on a limb. Fly it in that vacant lot on the corner where there are no trees."

The girl headed for the vacant lot, and she managed to get the kite into the air. My, but it looked grand up there against the sky. It looked like a big red bird. Or a big red diamond. The girl felt it tug at the string in her hand.

After a while a friend came along. "Come on with me to the park," the friend said. "Suzie's going to be there, and we're going to play jacks."

THE KITE

Well, the girl with the kite forgot all about the trees in the park. She wrapped the kite string around her wrist and hurried to be with her friends. But she had no more than stepped through the park gate than she felt a hard tug on the kite string. Then she felt no tension at all. The string fell limply at her feet.

The girl was almost in tears as she went to get her dad to help get the kite down from a tree limb. Dad went to the park, but he couldn't help.

"It's too bad you forgot about the trees," Dad said, "but there's no use crying over a lost kite."

"I'm not crying." The girl managed a smile and said, "I lost the kite, but I still have the string."

"What can you do with the string?" her dad asked.

"Lots of things," the girl said. "I can use a piece of it for a shoelace in that shoe where the real lace broke. And we can use another piece of string to make a circle to mark the boundary of our jack game. And I can use another piece of it to tie my doll's suitcase shut. There are a lot of things I can do with the piece of string."

I try to think of this kite story whenever things go wrong in my life. The Bible tells us that all things work together for good, but sometimes that's hard to believe—especially when it rains on your picnic day, or when you break out with measles on your birthday. But even when unhappy things happen, you can usually find something good to be glad about. Whenever life snags your kite, remember that you will still have the string.

Sentence prayer: Our Father: We thank you for your constant care, and we ask you to help us always see the good in life. Amen.

What If Everybody Did?

Prop: *A picture of a spider web.*

Scientists tell us that no two spiders spin the same kind of web. The web is the spider's unique trademark. If something pokes a hole in this web the spider has to repair the damage immediately or the whole web may come apart.

Now you may be wondering what spider webs have to do with you. All the living things on earth have one thing in common with spiders. All living things exist in a web of environment. *Environment* is a big word, but I'm sure you've all heard it before. Environment means our surroundings.

If a plant or animal species is in danger of being wiped out by pollution or disease, that's very similar to the hole in the spider's web. Something has to be done about it. It's only in recent years that we humans have paid much attention to what was happening to the other creatures in the world. We didn't realize that the extinction of a plant or animal species made any important difference to us. But now scientists have learned that what can happen to other life forms can also happen to humans. In fact they predict that these same things will happen to humans. There are holes in our web of environment that must be repaired. As responsible citizens we'll help mend the web whenever we can.

One day my children brought home a library book entitled *What If Everybody Did?* As I remember it, the book was in rhyme, and it was cleverly done. In its humorous way it asked what would happen if everybody wrote in library books or forgot to make beds or left the cap off the toothpaste. What if everybody did?

Have you ever dropped a wastepaper on the ground? Most of us have done that at some time. It doesn't seem like a very big crime. But think of it this way. Imagine a million people dropping paper on the ground. That would be a big problem. It would be a big chore to clean up all that paper. What one person does is important.

The world is our web, and it's up to each of us to help keep it in repair. You can help. If you see empty cans and bottles lying where they shouldn't be, put them in a trash bin. If you know of a group that recycles old papers, take yours to them. What if everybody did these things? Why the world would be a cleaner place for us to live in. Of course you can help. What if everybody did?

Sentence prayer: Our Father: Help us, the everybodys of this world, to do our best to keep our environment clean. Amen.

Piggy-Bank Minds

Prop: *A piggy bank.*

How many of you have piggy banks at home? Or maybe your bank is shaped differently. It doesn't matter. No matter what the shape of a bank, it serves one purpose. It holds coins. And where do the coins come from? Some are gifts, aren't they? Sometimes a grandmother or a grandfather or an aunt or uncle will drop a nickle or two in your bank.

Some coins are earned. You all know that. Maybe you earn a dime for running an errand or for doing some special job around the house. Probably those coins go into the bank. Sometimes certain coins are worth more to you than others. Of course you know that dimes are worth more than pennies. That's not what I mean.

Suppose you have two dimes. Maybe your aunt gave you one dime, and maybe you earned the other. Which dime means more to you? My guess is that you may take the gift dime and spend it on the first thing that catches your eye. But what about that dime you earned? Isn't it a little harder to spend? Do you remember that you walked six blocks to the store and six blocks back and that on the return trip you carried a gallon of milk that weighed about eight pounds? You earned that dime! You'll have to think a while before you spend it.

Sometimes at night before you go to bed, do you ever empty your bank to see what's in it? I used to do that. Sometimes my little brother would drop matchsticks into my bank. I'd throw those away. And sometimes my little sister would slip scraps of paper into my bank. I'd throw those away. But I'd keep the coins. They were valuable.

Have you ever stopped to think that our minds are a lot like piggy banks? The thoughts we drop into our minds might be compared to the coins we drop into a bank. Some thoughts are given to us by parents or teachers. And in all honesty, sometimes we don't value them too highly. "Eat your spinach." "Button your coat." "Stand up straight." But the thoughts are valuable, and they stay in our minds. Then there are the thoughts we earned through experience. Maybe a lump on the head taught us not to race indoors on a newly waxed floor. Then there are some worthless thoughts that slip into our minds that really don't belong there. Unkind thoughts. Selfish thoughts.

It might be a good idea to treat our minds like banks and empty them each night. This would give us a chance to think about the thoughts that were given to us and about the thoughts we earned through experience. And it would give us a chance to throw away worthless thoughts. This week let's think about our mind-banks and try to keep in them only thoughts of value.

Sentence prayer: Our Father: We thank you for our minds, and we ask your guidance in using them for the good of the world. Amen.

Surprise Package

Prop: *A wrapped gift box.*

How many of you like to receive presents? Of course! We all like presents, especially presents that are wrapped up and tied with a bow. Those are really nice because they're surprise gifts.

When I was young I once said, "Mom, I wish every day was Christmas. I'd like to get a present every day of the year."

And do you know what Mom said? She said, "Every day can't be Christmas, but you do receive a surprise gift every day of the year."

"You're kidding," I said. "What did I receive today?"

"The dawn," Mother said.

"The dawn?" I asked.

"Certainly," Mother said. "Dawn is the gift of a new day. And each new day is a surprise package. It's yours to do with as you choose."

I didn't say any more about wanting every day to be Christmas, but I thought a lot about each day being a surprise gift. The more I thought about the idea, the more truth it seemed to hold. We may think that today is just like yesterday, but it isn't.

Each new day can be a challenge to us. It can challenge us to do our best. Yesterday's mistakes

88

are past. We've learned from them, remembering their lessons and forgetting their sadnesses. We are wiser today than we were yesterday.

Each day offers us the gift of a new beginning. The new day offers us the chance to give thanks for our many blessings. You might want to begin each day with the thought "Today I am going to succeed." Now success will mean different things to different people. Maybe today you're going to succeed at making a new friend. Or maybe you are going to succeed in getting all your spelling words down correctly. Or maybe you're going to succeed at doing something nice for somebody else.

But whatever your goal, remember that the new day is your special gift. Enjoy it. Make the most of it. Make your gift count for something good.

Sentence prayer: Our Father: We thank you for the gift of each new day. Help us to use it for good. Amen.

The Line of Truth

Props: *A piece of string and two sticks.*

How many of you are sometimes tempted to tell a lie? You don't have to answer out loud, but think the answer to yourself. Did you ever wonder why it sometimes seems so much easier to tell a lie than to tell the truth? I think we've all wondered about that.

Suppose you broke a window with your ball. You know the consequences. Someone is going to scold. Someone is going to forbid you to play ball in that spot again. You're going to have to apologize to the person whose window you broke. And you're going to have to pay the cost of replacing the glass. Now, none of those are very pleasant things.

It would be a lot easier to say that some other person broke the window and ran off without leaving his name. You'd be off the hook. No apologies, no payment for new glass, no scolding. So you may wonder why it's wrong to lie. Maybe I can give you some ideas to think about.

You're familiar with these things I've brought with me today—a string and two sticks. You may wonder what they have to do with truth or lies. Can you think of what a person might use two sticks and a string for?

Do your parents ever plant a garden? Do you

ever see them tie a string to a stick on one side of the garden, stretch the string across the plowed ground, then tie it to a stick on the other side of the garden? Why did they do that? That's right. To make a straight row for planting seeds.

Now I like to think of this line marked by the string as the line of truth. Along this line the planted seeds are going to grow. Good things grow along the line of truth. But what grows to either side of the string? Weeds. Thistles. Burrs. To me these weeds represent lies and the confusion that is the result of lies.

Consider what happens to the weeds. The good gardener chops them down and gets rid of them. He has to work hard to keep his line of truth growing, to protect it from the weed growth that threatens from the sides. And the more successful the gardener is at fighting the weeds, the happier he will be about his harvest.

Whenever you are faced with the decision of whether to tell the truth or a lie, remember the two sticks and the string. If you keep your words directed along the line of truth, you will have earned a happy harvest.

Sentence prayer: Our Father: Guide us always toward speaking the truth. Amen.

A Ray of Sunshine

Prop: *A toy cat.*

You all know what this is. It's a toy cat. How many of you have pet cats at home? I used to have a cat when I was your age, and he was fun to watch. You know what he liked to do? Well, we had a big window in our living room that let a lot of sunshine into the house. My cat's favorite pastime was sleeping in the patch of sunshine that came in through the window.

Have you ever watched a patch of sunshine? If you've noticed, it moves. Slowly but surely it moves as the earth turns. Now my cat wasn't smart enough to know this. But whenever he got chilly, he'd open one eye, notice that his patch of sunshine had moved, and move himself back into it. Then he'd go back to sleep again.

When I was your age I sometimes wondered if God was angry with me when I was bad. Do you ever wonder about that? You know God wants you to be good. But when you don't quite measure up, how does he feel toward you? Does he shut his love off from you?

I don't think so. I think God's love is a lot like a patch of sunshine. It's warm and pleasant, and it's always there. Yes, even on a cloudy day that sunshine is there somewhere behind the clouds. But your world turns, and you have to learn to cope with its turning. If you do the right thing, you'll keep in the sunshine of God's smile. But once in a while you're going to make some mistakes. Everybody makes mistakes. And when you make a mistake you may feel as if you've been left out in the cold. You may feel that God doesn't love you, or that he's angry at you.

If this happens to you, the thing to remember is that the sunshine of God's love is always present. All you have to do is move yourself back into it. You may have to change your ways. You may have to change your beliefs. And sometimes this won't be easy. But no matter what troubles you face, God's love, like the sunshine, is always there.

Sentence prayer: Our Father: Thank you for your ever-present love and for helping us walk in its warmth. Amen.

A Time to Pray

Prop: *A homemade parachute.*

How many of you have ever made a toy parachute? It's easy to make. Just tie the four corners of a handkerchief together and add a weight. A fishing sinker will do. Or if you don't have a fishing weight, you may use a small rock that you can tie to the handkerchief corners.

After you toss your parachute up, it will fill with air and float to the ground. Toy parachutes are fun to play with. Real parachutes are used for a more serious purpose. Flyers use them to float safely to earth if something happens to their airplane and they find themselves in trouble high above the earth.

Few of us have the opportunity to fly in an airplane very often, but many times some of us try to use a parachute. We try to use prayer as a parachute. Did you ever think of that? Sometimes we forget to pray when everything's going fine for us. But the minute we get in any kind of trouble we hunt for a prayer-parachute to hold us up.

Now we all know that prayer shouldn't be used as a parachute. We all know we should pray regularly, but sometimes it's hard to remember to do it. And sometimes we make up excuses for not praying. We may say we're not in the right place. Or we may say we're too busy. Or we may say that there are too many people around us.

It might be a good idea to ask ourselves to name the best time for prayer. I once heard of a man who joked that the only way to pray was standing on your head in a haystack at dawn. Now in a way this man turned out to be right. One dawn he fell headfirst from the top of the barn into a haystack. And he started praying. He was buried in the hay only a short time before rescuers arrived to pull him to safety.

Praying standing on your head in a haystack at dawn may be appropriate in some cases, but most people can find a better time and place for it. Some people find a quiet prayer time early in the morning, just before they get up. And some people find a quiet prayer time at night, just before they go to sleep. It's a good idea to choose a regular time to pray; but if you forget, remember that God is always listening. Pray anytime. But try not to use prayer as a parachute—something you pull out only in times of trouble.

Sentence prayer: Our Father: We thank you that we can talk to you at any time and know you are listening. Amen.

Wind Up the World

Prop: *A music box.*

How many of you have listened to a music box? How many of you have music boxes at home? Let's listen to this one. (Let the box play.) Now what do we do when the music box quits playing? Right. We wind it up.

I had a friend once who owned a whole collection of music boxes. She had big ones, little ones, fancy ones, plain ones. And each box played a different tune. All her music boxes had one thing in common: eventually they ran down and someone had to wind them up. This made me start thinking.

Have you ever thought that people are a lot like music boxes? They play their individual tunes over and over, but eventually they run down and have to be wound up again before they can play. It's easy to wind up a music box. All you have to do is turn a key. But it's harder to wind up a person.

If a person is all run down, he may need sleep to wind him up again. Or he may need food to make him feel like playing his individual tune once more. Or sometimes a person may just need appreciation. Did you ever think of that? Appreciation may be the key.

Have you ever tried very hard to do something

and had nobody notice? Maybe you even did that something very well, but still nobody noticed. Has that ever happened to you? Maybe you cleaned up your room and nobody noticed. Or maybe you combed your hair a new way that you thought was attractive and nobody noticed. How did you feel about what you had done? Did you feel sort of run down like the music box that needs to be wound up?

On the other hand, have you ever cleaned up your room and had your parents notice and say, "How nice your room looks today!" Then how did you feel? You felt good, didn't you? You felt wound up and ready to do something else worthwhile.

That's the way it is with everyone. Everyone likes to be appreciated. It winds them up. How about trying an experiment this week? Why don't you pretend you're a key? Why don't you see how many people you can wind up with your key of appreciation. If one of your friends looks especially nice, tell him so. If another friend does well in a game at recess, tell her so. You have the key. And that key is called appreciation.

Sentence prayer: Our Father: Help us to appreciate the good things other people do. Amen.

Seeds and Faith

Props: *Two small flowerpots, one with dirt but no plant, one with a plant.*

How many of you have ever tried to raise a plant from a seed? Good! What kind of a seed did you plant?

I'm going to tell you a story about Kevin and Jill and seeds and faith. Kevin and Jill were involved in a classroom science project. They were to plant bean seeds, and then they were to keep a record of when each seed sprouted, when it got leaves, and how tall it grew in one week.

Kevin and Jill prepared soil in pots. They planted the seeds. They watered them. Then came the hard part. They had to wait. A bean seed doesn't sprout overnight. Their teacher told them to be patient, that the seed would sprout when it was ready and not before.

Now Kevin and Jill could hardly wait to see that seed sprout. They ran to the pots several times that first day to look for a sprout, but they saw nothing. On the second morning, Kevin felt sure his bean seed would have sprouted during the night. He ran all the way to school, but when he checked his flowerpot, he still saw nothing but dirt. Jill's pot looked the same as his. He sighed. Waiting was hard.

On the third day, Kevin decided to poke into his pot and see what was happening under the dirt. He tried to talk Jill into doing that too, but she wouldn't do it. The teacher had said to be patient, to have faith.

Kevin waited until nobody was looking; then he dug up his bean seed. It looked almost as it had looked when he put it in the dirt. Maybe a little fatter. So he planted the seed again and tamped the dirt back over it.

On the fourth day, Kevin dug his seed up again. Now it had split open, and when he poked at it he broke off the tiny green shoot that was trying to come forth. Quickly he buried the seed; then he tried to talk Jill into digging up her seed. She wasn't interested.

On the fifth day that the children looked at their pots, several of them saw tiny green sprouts breaking through the soil. Kevin didn't see one in his pot. On the sixth day some more pots had sprouts. And by the seventh day every one had a bean sprout except Kevin. Kevin knew why. He had ruined his seed by being impatient.

Now, many of us are like Kevin. We're too impatient to have our way about things. We go poking around where we shouldn't. This coming week whenever we feel ourselves growing impatient about something, let's try to think about Kevin and the bean seed. Let's be patient, and let's have faith in God's creative power.

Sentence prayer: Our Father: We thank you for the mysteries of this world and for our ever-growing faith in your wisdom. Amen.

The Abalone Shell

Prop: *An abalone shell.*

This shell has a story behind it that I think you might like to hear. Now it isn't very pretty on this side, is it? But just look at the other side, the inside. It's full of beautiful colors. The inside is sometimes called mother-of-pearl.

Once I knew a boy named Bill who liked to visit the beach a lot. One day he and a group of other children decided to have a contest to see who could find the prettiest shell. Now there were lots of shells on that beach. There were scallops and cowries and angel wings. They weren't all perfect shells, but even the fragments were pretty.

Bill walked along the shore, picking up every shell he saw, planning to discard the ugly ones later. The important thing now was to find as many shells to choose from as he could.

Bill saw an abalone shell early in his search, but he just saw the outside of it and kicked it aside thinking it would never win a beauty contest. It was just plain gray and sort of lumpy and dirty looking. Nobody else picked it up either.

When it was almost time to go home, Bill stopped gathering shells. It was time to sort and make a decision. He had shells in all his pockets, in his cap,

101

and in his hands; and now he laid them out on a smooth stretch of sand and looked around for something to wash the shells in. They were covered with sand, which hid some of their color.

This was a well-kept beach. There were no old cups or cartons. Then Bill remembered that big shell he had seen. It would hold water. He rushed back to the spot where he had seen it, and luck was with him. It was still there. He grabbed it and dashed to the water. When he turned that shell over and really examined it, he knew his search had ended. Here was the prettiest shell in his collection.

Bill always remembered this experience. He told me that he discovered that people are like shells. The Bible tells us to love one another, but sometimes that's hard to do. We have strange little prejudices. Sometimes we just look at a person and say to ourselves, "I don't like that one." That's what Bill did to the abalone shell. He just saw the ugly exterior and ignored the rest of the shell completely. But when he got closer to it and studied it carefully, he found it really was beautiful. And it's the same way with people. Once you get close to them, once you study them, you'll find surprising things. Good things.

Sentence prayer: Our Father: Help us to find the true beauty in our differences. Amen.

The Bean Plant

Prop: *A flowerpot with a bean plant that was grown from a seed.*

I want to show you this plant. Does anyone know what kind of a plant it is? Sure! It's a bean plant, and I raised it from a seed. I planted the bean seed. I watered it. And in a week or so a bean plant began to grow.

Now I want to tell you a funny story. When I was a boy about your age, my schoolteacher guided her class on a science project. We were to plant bean seeds and record facts about them as they grew.

When I went home from school that night I told my parents that I was going to raise a pomegranate. I'd read about pomegranates in the Bible, and I thought they sounded a lot more interesting than beans. My parents were surprised, and they asked me where I'd gotten a pomegranate seed. I told them I had a bean seed, but I had decided to grow a pomegranate, not a bean. Well, my parents laughed, and this made me sort of angry. I didn't see why I couldn't raise a pomegranate if I decided to.

So, about a week or so passed, and our seeds began to sprout. And do you know what. My plant turned into a bean plant just like all the other kids' plants. I was disappointed, and when I told the teacher why, she didn't laugh. She just said, "Now

103

you've learned that if you plant a bean seed you get a bean plant. If you want a pomegranate plant you'll have to plant a pomegranate seed."

I learned a real lesson from that bean seed. It made me aware of the Bible verse that says, "As ye sow, so shall ye reap." If you plant bean seeds you get bean plants.

If you use your imagination you can imagine that lots of things are seeds. If you plant smiles, you get smiles in return. If you plant frowns and scowls, you'll get frowns and scowls in return. That's the way life works. It's what we call a natural law. So be careful what you plant as you live through your life. Plant only the things you want returned to you.

I hope you'll remember my story about the bean seed and the pomegranate plant that I didn't get. You just can't raise a pomegranate from a bean seed.

Sentence prayer: Our Father: Help us sow seeds of love and kindness in our garden of life. Amen.

What Would You Rather Be?

Prop: *A picture of a butterfly.*

I remember a teacher who asked her pupils what they would like to be if they could be something other than a human being. One boy wanted to be a racehorse, because he thought thoroughbreds lived exciting lives. One of the girls wanted to be an owl, because she thought owls were wise.

When the teacher asked me, I said I'd like to be a butterfly. All butterflies had to do was flit around freely and have fun, and in the process they made the people who watched them happy.

My teacher soon set me straight on a few facts. "Butterflies are free only within certain limits," she said.

"What limits?" I asked.

"They're committed to certain things. First, they are caterpillars, and this means they have to go through a great change to earn their wings. Then, once they are butterflies, they are committed to a long migrating journey that's essential to their lives."

"But all the rest of the time they're free to do as they please," I said.

"Perhaps," the teacher said. "But butterflies have no choice about their commitments. Their lives are preplanned for them. I think it's much more exciting to be a human and be able to choose one's own commitments."

"But it's hard to always choose correctly," I said.

"True," the teacher agreed. "Butterflies don't sit around worrying about whether or not they're popular with the crowd. They don't flit around in a tizzy over whether their clothes are as pretty as the next butterfly's clothes. I think that being sure of their commitments is the thing that makes them so free. What do you think?"

I thought about that for a long time; then I agreed. Sometimes I had certain commitments to fulfill. For instance, on Saturdays it was my job to take out the garbage, shake rugs, and sweep. Those were my commitments. If I did them first thing in the morning, I was free to do as I pleased for the rest of the day. But sometimes I didn't get right at those chores, and when I didn't they nagged at me all day, and I really didn't enjoy what I was doing. Has this ever happened to you?

At the end of our classroom discussion, the first boy still chose to be a racehorse; the girl still chose to be an owl; and I still chose to be a butterfly. But I had learned that a butterfly stands for restrictions as well as freedom and that the restrictions make the freedom more enjoyable.

Sentence prayer: Our Father: Help us to earn freedom by choosing Christian commitments as we go through life. Amen.

The Still, Small Voice

Prop: *A conch shell.*

This is a conch shell, and it's found in tropical ocean waters. I'm going to pass it around for you to look at, and I want you to hold it to your ear like this. (Demonstrate.) The sound you hear may remind you of the roar of the ocean. Or it may sound like something else. I'm going to tell you a story about a girl who heard something besides ocean sounds when she put a conch shell to her ear.

Now while this girl was out playing on the beach early one morning, she found a purse with fifty dollars in it. She wanted to keep that money. Her aunt was sick, and she had heard her parents talking about the cost of medicine. She thought that fifty dollars could buy medicine that would help make her aunt well again.

The girl kept counting the money over and over again. At last she made herself look inside the purse more carefully. She smiled. There was no name in the purse. Surely she had a right to keep it, didn't she? She sat beside the surf and tried not to think of the lost-and-found box at the beach shop. She knew the man who ran the shop. If she turned the purse in, he would put it in the lost-and-found box. But the purse had no name in it. Someone might claim it who really hadn't lost it. That wouldn't be fair.

The girl thought for a long time, and while she was thinking she picked up an old conch shell that had washed onto the beach. It wasn't pretty and shiny like this one. It was dull and chipped, but when she held it to her ear, it spoke to her. At first she heard ocean sounds, but soon she seemed to hear a small voice telling her to turn the money in at the beach shop.

Taking the shell and the purse the girl ran to the shop. The man in charge thanked her and told her that if nobody claimed the money within thirty days, she could have it for her own. He assured her that anyone claiming it would have to identify the purse correctly and know the amount and number of bills that it contained.

After thirty days nobody had claimed the money, and the girl got to keep it. Of course she was happy, but it made her feel good to know that she had done the right thing. For years she kept that conch shell, and whenever she had a problem, she would listen to the small voice in the shell before she made a decision.

I don't really believe that the voice the girl heard came from within the shell, do you? I think it came from within that girl herself. Conch shells are fun to listen to, but it's good to know that we can all listen to the still, small voice within each of us.

Sentence prayer: Our Father: Thank you for the still, small voice within each of us, and tune our ears that we may always be able to hear it. Amen.

Persistence

Prop: *A picture of an orange marigold and a yellow marigold.*

How many of you know what kind of flower this is? Right. It's a marigold. Maybe you've seen blossoms like these in your mother's garden or your grandmother's flower bed. For many years marigolds only bloomed in these two colors.

Orange and yellow marigolds are pretty, but about twenty years ago the president of a big seed company decided that he wanted to develop a white marigold, and he wanted it to be at least two-and-one-half inches across.

That was quite a wish. How would anyone go about getting a white marigold when seeds were available for orange and yellow only? This seed man asked gardeners all over the country to help develop a white marigold. He offered a prize and invited anyone who was interested in trying to develop a white marigold blossom to submit seeds to his company.

A lady in Iowa thought it would be interesting to try to develop a white marigold. Do you know how she went about it? First she planted seeds from yellow marigolds. When they bloomed she studied the blossoms and tied a red string around the blossom stems that were lightest in color. When

111

those blossoms withered, she saved seed from them. Then she had to wait until the next spring to plant the seed, wait for the plants to grow and bloom. And the next year the marigolds were still yellow. But some of them were a lighter yellow, and the lady marked the lightest blossoms with red string and saved seed from them for the next year's planting.

Do you know how many years she did this? Twenty years! A lot of people would have given up after one or two years. Or even three or four years. But this woman kept trying for a white marigold for twenty years, and at last she developed one. She won the prize from the seed company, but what was even more important, she gave the world a new kind of flower.

Most of us know that the Bible tells us to seek and we will find, to knock and doors will be opened to us; but many times we expect this to happen too soon. Haven't you all wanted something very badly? Maybe you've prayed for it, but you still haven't gotten it. If that happens to you, I hope you'll remember that the Bible doesn't say when you'll find what you seek. It doesn't say when the doors will be opened to your knock.

Many times people give up seeking and knocking too soon. They expect things to come too easily. If the time ever arrives when you feel disappointed in your efforts to achieve something, I hope you'll remember the story of the white marigold and the lady who kept seeking and knocking for twenty long years.

Sentence prayer: Our Father: Thank you for your promise that if we'll seek we'll find. Amen.

What'll I Do Now?

Prop: *Swim flippers or a swim mask.*

Many of you are probably thinking about summer vacation. What will you do this summer? Camp? Swim? Picnic? I used to look forward to summer when I was your age. Swimming was my thing. Sometimes I used this (hold up prop) to help. During the first few days of vacation I swam many hours. But before long I was running to my mother and saying, "What'll I do now, Mom? I don't have anything to do."

Do you ever say that to your folks? What happened to all those marvelous vacation dreams? I'll tell you. Nothing really happened to them. They're still around. But when you start asking, "What'll I do now, Mom?" you've learned that it's just as boring to play all the time as it is to work all the time. Life should be a mixture of work and play.

If you're thinking that you're too young to work at a regular job, you're right. And you're lucky. You have time to start learning to be an expert. You know what an expert is? An expert is a person who has great knowledge in a certain area. There are experts in the field of medicine. They may know all about one certain disease. Other experts are in the field of astronomy. They know all about certain stars. People look up to experts because they have such vast knowledge about their chosen field.

If you'd like to be an expert, summer vacation is a good time to start. You can be an expert in whatever field you choose.

Once I knew a boy who was interested in maps. During the summer he studied about maps. Now he didn't bury himself in the library, and he didn't always have his nose in a book. But every day he spent a few minutes learning about maps. One of the interesting things that happened to him while he was still in elementary school was that he found an error on a map published by a famous company. He wrote to the company, and the president acknowledged their error. They corrected the mistake in their next edition, and they sent this boy a free atlas as a thank you for his help.

I read about a Japanese boy who spent a little time every night studying the stars, and an exciting thing happened to him. He discovered a comet that nobody else had noticed. The astronomers of the world agreed to name the comet after him. How would you like to have a star named after you? It could happen.

Why not experiment this summer? Spend a few minutes each day reading about your own special interest. You may want to keep a notebook. Not only will you be on your way to becoming an expert, but you may also be giving yourself a headstart into pursuing what may become a fascinating career when you're older. Use this world the Creator has given you, and I guarantee that you'll have little need to say, "Mom, what'll I do now?"

Sentence prayer: Our Father: Thank you for vacation-time. Amen.

Combinations

Props: *Alphabet blocks. A card bearing the word Fight. One card bearing the letter* L.

I'm sure you all know about alphabet blocks. They're something you played with when you were much younger. You probably had a set of all twenty-six letters. Did you ever stop to think about the alphabet? Twenty-six letters! That's really not very many. But think of the thousands of words we can make by using different combinations of these letters. We can make kind words or cruel words, words of love or words of hate. The choice is ours.

For instance, look at this word. (Hold up the Fight card.) It's really more of a hate word than a love word, isn't it? But look what happens when you change just one letter. (Put the *L* over the *F*.) Now we have *Light* instead of *Fight*. It's that easy.

Think of all the people in this world of ours. There are only twenty-six alphabet letters in our language, but there are millions of people in the world. In a way, people make up a world alphabet. People can be put in endless combinations. And combinations of people can spell kind acts or cruel acts, acts of love or acts of hate.

When we're working with letters, we can choose the words we want to use. By using only kind words we set an example for others. But when we're working with combinations of people, the choice of group action isn't all up to us. All we can do is set an example. If you find yourself involved in a combination of people who suddenly start to poke fun at someone, you know that this is an unkind act. What can you do about it?

You're just one person, just one of the group. But remember the words *fight* and *light*. Just one part of a combination can change things. You're the one who can stand up for the person being picked on. There's a good chance that your words and actions can change the combination of your group.

Whenever you meet a situation that threatens to shift from kindness to cruelty, see if you can't be the person who can change the combination back to kindness. People working together can create miracles.

Sentence prayer: Our Father: We thank you for the importance of individuals working together for good. Amen.

Good Times

Props: *A picnic basket and a blanket.*

If you were going on a picnic (show picnic basket), there would be certain things that you'd take along, right? You'd probably want some sandwiches, maybe some deviled eggs, perhaps some soda pop (you may want to show these things also), and you'd probably need a blanket (show prop) to sit on while you ate lunch.

And if you're going to school, there are certain things you'll take along. You'll need a pencil and paper. You'll need books. Perhaps a ruler is essential. Or some scissors. The important thing is that you take the things that you need with you. You don't expect someone else to bring them for you.

But there is one thing that we frequently forget to take with us whether we're going to school, to a picnic, or just to run an errand. Can you guess what we sometimes forget? Sometimes we forget to take our good times with us. That's right. Our good times.

Once at a picnic I overheard a small boy rush up to his dad and say, "But I'm not having any fun." I was interested in hearing what the father would answer. And I soon learned that he was very wise. He didn't get all excited. He didn't drop what he

119

was doing and entertain his son. He didn't give him money and tell him to buy an ice-cream cone or a balloon. He merely looked at him and said, "Maybe you forgot to bring your fun with you."

The child looked surprised for a moment; then he smiled. I guessed that this was something they had talked over at home in the past. The boy thought a moment, then said, "I think I'll get the kids together and tell ghost stories."

"Good idea," his father agreed.

Bring your good times with you. That's really a wonderful idea. Maybe you can't always carry a toy in your pocket, but you can carry interesting thoughts in your mind. These thoughts are your good times. Think about things you've always wondered about. Leaves, for instance. How many kinds do you suppose there are? Birds. How many kinds can you name. And stories. Everybody likes to hear a good story. Christ often told people to rejoice. He wants you to be happy, and the way to be happy is to decide to be happy and to take your good times with you wherever you go.

Sentence prayer: Our Father: Thank you for the ability to rejoice in the wonderful world you have given us. Amen.

The Sand Dollar

Prop: *A sand dollar.*

Do you know what this is? Some of you may know. It's a seashell called a sand dollar. Sand dollars are rather hard to find, but once when I was about your age I was going on a beach vacation and I was determined to find one.

The vacation site was Padre Island, Texas, and I knew there were sand dollars to be found in that area because I had seen some specimens in the park ranger's station.

I wondered if sand dollars washed in on the high tide or the low tide. But it didn't really matter. I would be at the beach only a short time; I had to use the tide that was there. For a couple of days I searched in the loose sand far back from the water, but I found nothing. On the third day I stood at the water's edge and waited for a sand dollar to wash in at my feet. Again, no luck. And my time was running out. Soon we would have to leave the beach and go home.

I had a feeling that there were sand dollars out in

that water and that I could find one if I just had the courage to step in. But the water was cold. And it rushed toward me in great frothy waves. To get right down to facts, I was afraid to put a toe in that water. Have you ever felt that way?

Well, that's the way I felt. Afraid. If a sand dollar washed in at my feet, fine. But I was afraid to risk going into the water after one. But at last I saw that if I was going to find a sand dollar, I was going to have to go after it. I waded into the water. It was quite shallow near the shore, and it wasn't as scary as I had imagined. The waves swirled in knee deep, but then they receded and the water barely reached my ankles. Then I noticed something.

When the waves went out I was left standing in a shallow pool. I looked down through the clear water at the sand, and, sure enough, there was a sand dollar. I picked it up before it washed out with the next wave.

I've kept this sand dollar in my desk drawer for many years because I learned something from it. We all want friends, but sometimes we're afraid to get our feet wet by going out of our way to meet people. Whenever I feel this way I think about this shell. Friends won't wash in on the tide and lie at your feet. You have to plunge into the surf and go meet them. But if you take the first step, the rest will be easier. Most people want friends as badly as you do.

The next time you're around a group of people,

don't be afraid. Think about this sand dollar, and wade right in to see how many friends you can find.

Sentence prayer: Our Father: We thank you for our many opportunities to meet new friends, knowing you will give us courage to take the first step. Amen.

Something for Nothing

Prop: *A silver dollar.*

As a minister I spend quite a bit of time visiting with parents and teachers, and many times our talk is about children and what makes them unhappy or happy. People tell me that often their children worry because they think they have no friends. Is this true? Do you ever feel that you have no friends?

As I think back on it, I used to feel this way too sometimes. I felt that nobody really liked me. My ears stuck out. I was too fat. My clothes weren't what the in-crowd was wearing. One day I mentioned all this to my grandfather, and he listened patiently to me. Then he told me a secret that I'm going to pass on to you.

Do you see this coin I have here? Take a look. Sure, it's real. A silver dollar. You don't see these around much anymore. Now if I told you that tomorrow morning at ten o'clock there would be a man on Main Street passing out free silver dollars, would you believe me?

You might want to believe me, but down deep in your heart you'd know that nobody would give away silver dollars. If you asked your parents about it, they might laugh and tell you that you can't get something for nothing. This is a truth that you may hear many times during your life. You can't get something for nothing.

But like all great truths these words can be turned around. Reverse them, and you'll have a truth that may be even more helpful to you. If you can't get something for nothing, then it stands to reason that you can't give something without getting something for it in return. Ever think of that?

Let's think about that truth and how it works in our lives. What does a store do before it gets customers? It gives service, courtesy, and a square deal. What do your parents do before they can get their paychecks? They give of their work, don't they? They can't get a paycheck for nothing, but when they give something, they receive something. What does a farmer do before he gets a crop of corn? He gives the seed to the ground.

If you apply this truth to friendship, you'll know that you can't get a friend for nothing. But if first you give friendship to someone, you'll get friendship in return. Try out this truth this week, and see if it doesn't work for you. And don't feel sad that you can't get something for nothing. Instead be glad that by giving something you'll get something in return.

Sentence prayer: Our Father: Thank you for universal truths and for your help in understanding them. Amen.

The Gift
of Free Will

Prop: *A puppet.*

Do you ever feel as if you hear too much about being good? Do you ever wonder why if God wants you to be good he doesn't make you good? I used to feel that way when I was your age. When I started off for school in the morning the last thing my mother always said to me was, "Now, be good today." When I sat down at the table, someone usually said, "Now be good and eat your carrots." And always before I went to a birthday party my mother reminded me to be good.

Do people say things like that to you? They do? And it isn't easy to be good, is it? You have to think a lot about it when you'd rather be thinking of other things. If God wanted you to be good, why didn't he make you good? After all, he's the creator.

I've brought a friend with me here today. (Bring out the puppet.) How many of you have played with a puppet? It's fun, isn't it? You pull a string, and an arm moves. You pull another string, and a leg moves. You pull yet another string, and the head nods. But after a while a person gets tired of pulling strings, and he turns to more interesting things. Would you like to be a puppet?

Being a puppet might be fun for a while. You'd

never have to think, because someone else would be pulling your strings and ordering your actions. Maybe you'd want to wave to a friend, but if the puppeteer wanted you to tie your shoe instead, that's what you'd do. The puppeteer would be your boss. You wouldn't have to use your brains at all.

But don't you think that would soon get boring? If you didn't have a brain you might be able to go along with being a puppet. But you do have a brain. And the fact that you have a brain is one of the most exciting things about you.

You're no puppet. Nobody can decide your actions for you. You were born with free will. You are allowed to choose between good and bad. This adds to the excitement of your life. If God had created you good, you would be like a puppet. But God gave you free will, and he's given you a lifetime to learn to use your gift.

Give thanks that you have free will and a brain to help you make right decisions. And you might also give thanks that you have parents and teachers who love you enough to remind you to—you guessed it—be good. They are helping you learn to use your free will in the best possible way.

Sentence prayer: Our Father: We thank you for the gift of free will and for your help in teaching how to use it wisely. Amen.